S0-ABA-924

DISCARD

Humphrey
the Wrong
Way Whale

052462

Kathryn Allen Goldner
and Carole Garbuny Vogel

DILLON PRESS
Minneapolis, Minnesota 55415

Photographic Acknowledgments

The following people generously provided many excellent photographs: Cynthia D'Vincent, of Ocean Research Under Sail; Kenneth C. Balcomb, III; Dr. Tom Ford, Jr.; and William F. Dolphin, of Boston University.

Photographs were also provided by the Pacific Whale Foundation; the California Office of Tourism; Dr. John A. K. Davies; the Kendall Whaling Museum; Mason Weinrich, Cetacean Research Unit of the Gloucester Fishermen's Museum; Greenpeace; the Hawaii Visitors Bureau; Marineland of Florida; the Massachusetts Tourism Division; the Old Dartmouth Historical Society Whaling Museum; Prudence Stuhr; Bob Wilson of the California Marine Mammal Center; and Allen A. Wolman of the National Marine Mammal Laboratory.

Library of Congress Cataloging in Publication Data

Goldner, Kathryn Allen.
  Humphrey, the wrong-way whale.
  (Ocean world library)
  Bibliography: p.
  Includes index.
  Summary: Introduces information on the behavior and current situation of humpback whales through the story of an individual whale off the coast of California.
  1. Humphrey (Whale)—Juvenile literature. 2. Humpback whale—Biography—Juvenile literature. [1. Humphrey (Whale) 2. Humpback whale. 3. Whales]
I. Vogel, Carole Garbuny. II. Title. III. Series.
QL737.C424G65 1987   559.5'1   86-29332
ISBN 0-87518-360-3

Dillon Press, Inc., 242 Portland Avenue South
Minneapolis, Minnesota 55415

Printed in the United States of America
  2 3 4 5 6 7 8 9 10 96 95 94 93 92 91 90 89 88

Contents

Acknowledgments

Without the help of the community of whale researchers and whale lovers, we would have been unable to write this book. We would especially like to thank the following people for taking time to share information with us and for having the patience to read and comment on our manuscript: Peigin C. Barrett, executive director of the California Marine Mammal Center; Kevin C. Chu, Ph.D., of the Ocean Research and Education Society; William F. Dolphin, Ph.D., of Boston University; Linda Guinee, of the Long-Term Research Institute; Scott D. Kraus, of the New England Aquarium; and Robert L. Webb, of the Kendall Whaling Museum.

We are also indebted to the following people for their time and help: Cynthia D'Vincent, of Ocean Research Under Sail; Dr. Tom Ford, Jr., Patricia M. Harcourt, of the Ocean Research and Education Society; Judy Perkins and Victoria Rowntree, of the Long-Term Research Institute; and Dave Witrow and Allen A. Wolman, of the National Marine Mammal Laboratory.

Many other people provided us with up-to-date information in their fields of expertise: Robbins Barstow, Ph.D., and Kate O'Connell, of Cetacean Society International; Jon Lien, Ph.D., of Memorial University of Newfoundland; Marilyn K. Marx, of the Center for Coastal Studies; and Gregory K. Silber, of the University of California at Santa Cruz.

We would also like to acknowledge the help of Katrynka North Adachi, Robert H. Ellis, Jr. and Stuart M. Frank of the Kendall Whaling Museum; Patricia M. Fiorelli, formerly of the New England Aquarium; Dr. Nancy Foster, of the Sanctuary Programs Division, NOAA; Louis M. Herman, Ph.D., of the University of Hawaii; Steve King, of The Whale Fund; Marc Osten and Jay Townsend of Greenpeace; David Schmid, of Marineland of Florida; H. Sheridan Stone, of the National Marine Fisheries Service; and the U.S. Coast Guard, Rio Vista, California, Station.

We would like to acknowledge the help of many other people who helped us, either directly or indirectly. Where the opinions of experts conflicted, we used our own judgment in presenting the information. We take full and final responsibility for the accuracy of our work.

We are grateful to the members of our writers' group—Mary D. Bailey, Edith Gilmore, Ph.D., Linda McCabe, P. K. Slone, and Phyllis Whitman—for listening to revision after revision of our manuscript and offering helpful criticism. Special thanks go to our husbands and our children for their understanding.

Humpback Whale Facts

Maximum Size in Recent Years:
53 feet (16 meters) and about 50 tons (45 metric tons)

Humpback Whale Food:
Krill; schooling fish up to 12 inches (31 centimeters) in length

Calving and Breeding Grounds:
Warm tropical waters near the equator

Feeding Grounds:
Usually cold waters near the poles

Estimated Worldwide Population:
15,000-20,000

Whale Protection:
Fully protected from hunting since 1985

Greatest Threats to Survival:
Ocean pollution; competition with humans for food

Reproductive Cycle:
Females bear young every 1 to 4 years; usually every 2 to 3 years

Life Span:
30 to 50 years or more

 A Calf Is Born

The pregnant humpback searched the coastline of the tropical island. It was late fall. She had recently completed her journey from the distant feeding grounds. For eleven months her unborn **calf*** had been growing within her. Now, birthing time neared.

Behind a coral reef, the whale sought shelter in a shallow lagoon. Here, the warm water teemed with life. Brightly colored fish darted among the coral. Snails and starfish hid in its nooks and crannies.

The female humpback floated on her back. Up and down, back and forth, the bus-sized **mammal** twisted the lower part of her body. She rolled over to breathe through her paired **blowholes**. Then she turned again on her back. The whale waved her flippers in the air. She slapped the water with her tail **flukes**.

As she labored, she heard the sounds of other whales. Dolphins clicked and fish grunted. The hum of motor boats added to the underwater symphony.

Before long, a calf, later to be known as Hum-

---

*Words in **bold type** are explained in the glossary at the end of this book.

Shallow lagoons provide shelter for humpback mothers and their calves.
(Bob Abraham)

phrey, came out of the **cow's** body. The mother helped her newborn to the surface. Humphrey pushed the top of his head out of the water. He took his first breath, and then another. A fine mist spouted from his blowholes.

The baby whale weighed about 1,500 pounds (681 kilograms). He measured 14 feet (4.3 meters), the length of a compact car. His flukes and dorsal fin were curled from their tight position inside his mother. His

Round knobs dot the jaws of a humpback whale. (Kenneth C. Balcomb)

back and head were a light gray that would darken with age. No **barnacles** or scars speckled his body.

Except for these features, Humphrey looked like a small version of the older whale. Round knobs dotted his upper jaw and snout. Parallel folds ran from his chin to his navel. A fin jutted from his back and long white flippers extended from his sides. On his belly, the skin was white.

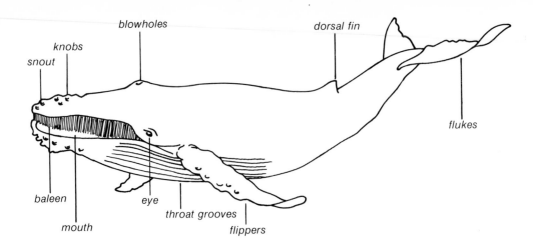

This diagram shows the parts of a humpback whale.

Feeling hungry, Humphrey dove beneath his mother. With his mouth, he prodded the cow's body. Between her flippers and the base of her tail, he located one of two small slits. He poked it, and a nipple popped out. Humphrey grasped the nipple in his mouth. Muscles inside his mother's hidden mammary gland squirted out thick warm milk. As the young whale nursed awkwardly, he swallowed sea water. Some of the milk dribbled away.

Within a few hours, Humphrey's wrinkled fin and flukes became stiff and straight. Within a few days, the young humpback could gulp 3 gallons (11.3 liters) of milk in less than a minute. Each day Humphrey drank enough to fill a bathtub—about 120 gallons (453.6 liters). The milk was rich in fat and protein and provided the **nutrients** for the calf to gain 50 pounds (22.7 kilograms) each day. It quickly thickened his **blubber**, the blanket of fat under the skin.

Slowly, the cow and calf moved through the shallow water near the coastline. A dolphin joined them.

With a graceful rolling action, the cow surfaced to breathe. Humphrey tried to copy his mother.

A whalewatch boat cruised offshore. When Humphrey approached it, the cow swam between the vessel and her calf. She led Humphrey away, but the dolphin stayed behind.

Like other newborn humpbacks, Humphrey had a favorite swimming position. He stayed above his mother's head or one of her flippers. Since he could not dive deeply, the cow remained near the surface. There, Humphrey swam easily by waving his flukes. But he was neither as fast nor as graceful as the cow. To keep up, he pumped his tail twice for each stroke of hers. When he tired, Humphrey rested beside his mother.

The pair stopped often. During these pauses, Humphrey surfaced and breathed three or four times. Then he dove, but not very deep. Sometimes, the baby whale twirled around and swam upside down. He used his mother's head as a slide and slipped down it. She held him in her flipper much like a human mother cradles her infant.

The young calf imitated his mother. When she flung her head out of the water, Humphrey flung his. When the cow slapped the surface with her flippers or tail, Humphrey slapped the surface, too. When she **breached**, so did Humphrey. One after the other, they thundered halfway out of the water. They twisted their bodies in midair, and crashed back into the sea.

Fit for the Sea

Humphrey is a real whale that became famous as an adult. No one followed him through life, but he probably developed like other humpbacks. This story of Humphrey's birth and growth is based on what scientists know about humpback whales.

Humpbacks are adapted for life in the sea. They use their paddlelike flippers for steering and balance. The bones inside each flipper are like those of a human arm and hand, but much bigger. The whales' bulging eyes are protected by a thick, skinlike layer, or membrane. The necks of humpbacks are so short that their heads appear to be connected directly to their bodies. Fishlike in shape, whales have few hairs. They have no hind legs, and no visible ears. Because of this **streamlining**, water glides smoothly over their bodies.

Humpbacks are not fish. Like other whales, they are mammals and must come to the surface to breathe air. When a humpback **blows**, a spout can be seen.

When breaching, a humpback often leaps from the water on its side. Waving its flippers, the whale twists in the air and lands on its back. (Kenneth C. Balcomb)

A clear, skinlike layer protects a humpback's bulging eyes. (Kenneth C. Balcomb)

Scientists disagree about what is in the spout. Some think it begins as seawater trapped in the rims above the blowholes. The whale's breath blasts the water upward into a spray. Others believe the spout also contains water vapor from the lungs. As it hits the cooler ocean air, it condenses. People experience the same thing on cold days when their breath is visible. Still other scientists think the humpback's spout has a

A humpback whale breathes through two blowholes located on its back. (Dr. Tom Ford, Jr.)

third element—an oily mucus from the windpipe. They think the humpback "coughs" out this mucus in much the same way you clear your throat.

Whale Groups on the Breeding Grounds

A strong bond exists between a mother humpback and her calf. If the pair did not stay together, the baby would starve. Or it could be attacked by sharks or killer whales.

A herd of hundreds of whales shares the breeding grounds. Young, old, and in between, they spread out over a large area. Year-old calves stay with their mothers unless the cow has a new baby. Then the **yearling** remains nearby. Although each cow and calf pair stays together, they do not seem to join other pairs. Fathers apparently do not help raise their calves.

Except for cow and calf pairs, contacts between humpbacks last for short periods. The whales may travel alone. They may also form twosomes, or larger groups called **pods** that include as many as twenty humpbacks. These pods remain together for short periods. The whales move from one group to another, or swim off alone.

Little to Eat

The calm, sheltered waters of the tropics are ideal for raising young humpbacks. And yet, they provide little food for large whales. While here, adult humpbacks rarely eat. They live mostly off their blubber.

The blubber layer of a pregnant female can be seven inches (eighteen centimeters) thick when she

A humpback cow and calf move together gracefully underwater. (Pacific Whale Foundation)

leaves the polar feeding grounds. It provides her with enough energy to travel the long distance to the hump-back breeding grounds. It gives her nutrients to maintain her body and complete the growth of her unborn calf. It also provides nutrients to produce milk after the calf's birth. By the end of the winter, the cow has lost about a third of her body weight. Half her blubber is gone.

2 The Ungentle Giants

Humphrey and his mother swam slowly through open water. The sea heaved and fell in a smooth, silent roll. Behind and slightly below the pair traveled an adult male, an **escort**. He had joined them a few hours earlier. At a distance, another male hung slanted underwater. With his flippers outstretched, his head down and tail up, the lone humpback "sang." He moaned, groaned, screamed, clicked, whistled, snored, and yupped. His highest tones were cries and chirps. The lowest tones sounded eerie and haunting.

The **song** was a complex pattern of sounds. It lasted fifteen minutes, and then the whale sang it again. Humphrey, his mother, and her escort stayed away. While they swam through the breeding grounds, the singer repeated his song over and over. Surfacing only once in each song to breathe, he continued for hours. From several miles distant, Humphrey and the two adults heard the song. Finally, the sounds of motor boats and ships drowned out the singing whale.

An adult male humpback often escorts a cow and her calf. (Pacific Whale Foundation)

When Humphrey's pod returned to the area, the singer stopped singing. Racing toward the group, he challenged the escort. He hurled himself into the air. With a giant splash, he sank back down.

The escort raised his tail flukes. Violently, he slapped the surface. He dived in front of his challenger and released a stream of bubbles from his blowholes.

The newcomer slowed, his vision blocked by the

*Humpback males challenge each other for the right to be an escort.
(Pacific Whale Foundation)*

bubbles. Then, with a burst of speed he tried to outflank the escort. In the lead of the battling males, Humphrey's mother increased the pace. She zigzagged across the surface of the water. She zoomed toward a boat, then veered quickly away. Little Humphrey stroked his tail furiously to keep up.

The whales slowed. Lifting his head above water, the challenger lunged forward. He arched his back and gulped in air. His pleated throat expanded like an accordion. The challenger appeared larger and more threatening.

Lashing their tails, the rivals attacked each other with their chins. Water sprayed high above them. Blood flowed from the knobs on the escort's jaw. Wheezing sounds filled the air. Head on, the males crashed together and shot straight out of the water.

Suddenly, the fighting stopped. Defeated, the original escort swam off. The challenger remained as a new escort for Humphrey and his mother.

Giant Singers of the Deep

Scientists believe that probably only male humpbacks sing. A singing humpback produces its melody without vocal cords. It may create the sounds by moving air within the spaces in its head. Humpback songs are fixed patterns of sounds that last from two to thirty minutes. The songs are repeated for many hours. Spaced far apart in the breeding grounds, many humpbacks sing at the same time.

The whales all sing nearly the same song, but they do not sing in unison. Slowly and steadily, the song changes. What the humpbacks sing in January is not the same as what they sing in February or March. As the breeding season passes, each whale changes its song in the same way as every other whale. To keep up with the latest changes in the song, the singers learn from each other.

Humpbacks in breeding grounds throughout the eastern North Pacific Ocean sing the same song. The song changes in similar ways in Hawaiian waters and in other North Pacific breeding grounds thousands of miles away. The songs, however, don't carry far. Scientists do not know how the changes are communicated across the ocean during the breeding season.

As winter goes on, humpbacks sing more and more. In the spring, they gradually stop. During the summer on the feeding grounds, the whales do not sing. They start again in the fall before they migrate, singing the same song they sang at the end of the previous breeding season.

Researchers think humpbacks sing often enough on the feeding grounds and while migrating to maintain similar songs throughout the eastern North Pacific Ocean. Some humpbacks might visit more than one breeding ground each winter. They could carry the latest tune with them. Scientists know that some whales migrate to different breeding grounds in different years.

Humpbacks in the South Pacific Ocean and other regions are probably not in contact with humpbacks from the North Pacific. As a result, the song in each area is distinct.

Songs and Mating

The humpback calving season is also the mating season. To mate, males and females must find each other in their vast underwater **habitat**. Like humans, they cannot see far underwater. However, sound can travel great distances through water, and the hearing of humpbacks is good. Scientists believe songs might identify, locate, and communicate information about individual males. The female may choose her mate by his song. In humpback language the song may say to her, "Here I am. Come and get me."

Male humpbacks compete for the females. Some experts think the males form a **dominance order** with their songs. The dominance order is the ranking of the whales. It helps the humpbacks recognize which males are superior, and which are inferior, to themselves. By being aware of the higher dominance of others, less

North Atlantic Ocean

Asia

Europe

Africa

South
America

South Atlantic Ocean

Indian Ocean

Antarctic Ocean

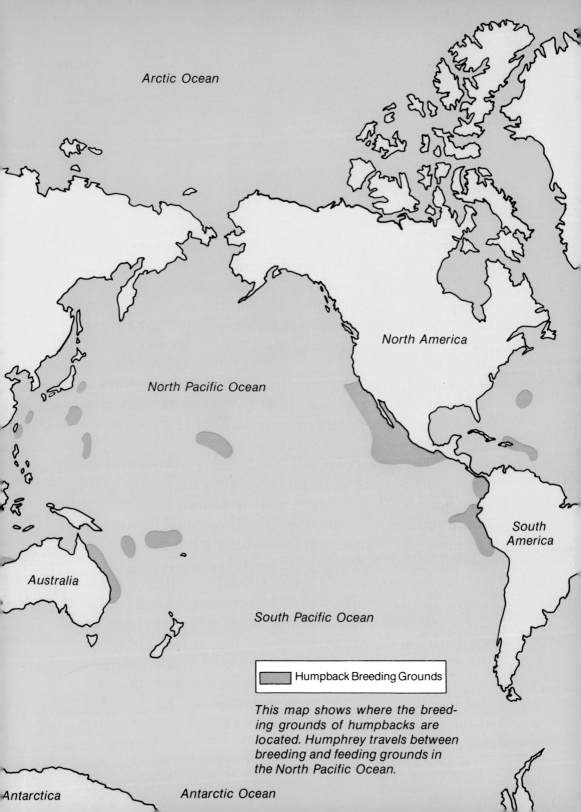

Arctic Ocean

North America

North Pacific Ocean

South America

Australia

South Pacific Ocean

Antarctica

Antarctic Ocean

Humpback Breeding Grounds

This map shows where the breeding grounds of humpbacks are located. Humphrey travels between breeding and feeding grounds in the North Pacific Ocean.

dominant males avoid fights. Challenges occur when the standing between rivals is not clear.

The length of time a male sings may tell how strong he is and how great his endurance. If so, a song from a strong male may say: "Here I am. Don't mess with me." When a young male hears it, he may decide to stay away.

Humpbacks also use threats to help form the social order. They breach, bubble, and slap the water with their flippers and flukes. Such actions may scare off rivals.

When a male challenges another, the two whales fight hard. In the past, humpbacks were called "gentle giants." Tales of their gentleness came from swimmers and boaters who were neatly avoided by nearby whales. These stories are true, but do not give a complete picture. Fighting was mistaken for play.

Winners of fights keep or obtain positions as escorts. Until recently, adults escorting cows and calves were called "aunts." People believed they were females that helped defend and care for the calves. Recently, however, researchers have discovered that escorts are males. They think that becoming an escort increases a male's chance of mating with a cow.

Winners of fights keep or obtain positions as escorts. Throughout the breeding season, a cow has many different escorts. (Pacific Whale Foundation)

Throughout the breeding season, a cow has many different escorts. The escorts remain with her for a short time—from less than an hour to a few days. The males, in turn, accompany many females. More than one male may challenge an escort. In fact, as many as fifteen males at a time may pursue one cow and calf. Once in a while, two cows and two calves travel in the same pod.

Social Sounds

Songs are not the only sounds produced by humpbacks. These whales also make at least twenty-five different noises known as **social sounds**. Social sounds are produced in both the breeding and the feeding grounds. They are sudden, short bursts of sounds, often followed by long silences. Social sounds are mostly low in pitch. Unlike the sounds in songs, they are not repeated in long patterns.

Scientists have much to learn about social sounds. They are studying the relationships between the sounds and the behaviors of individuals. Some of the sounds go with certain behaviors. For example, a whale may make a wheezing sound while spouting, usually during a threat display. On the breeding grounds, social sounds are often heard among groups of humpbacks. They occur when adult males are making threats or fighting. The sounds may discourage rivals.

Since they were discovered, the sounds of humpback whales have fascinated people. Humpback songs have been included in musical compositions. They have been released on several recordings, one of which sold more than 100,000 copies. In 1977, two Voyager

spacecraft carried an unusual record. On it were
works of Bach, Mozart, and a rock group; greetings in
fifty-five languages; and a "welcoming message" from
a humpback whale. The recording was sent with the
hope that intelligent beings will find it and under-
stand at least one of the languages.

 Journey to the Feeding Grounds

In March humpbacks began to leave the warm waters of the breeding grounds. Alone or in small pods, the yearlings and adults without calves departed first. Humphrey, his mother, and the other cows with young remained under the hot tropical sun until late spring. By then, the calves had grown much stronger. They were ready to start their first **migration**, or journey, toward the cold northern feeding grounds. Humphrey and his mother were among the last to go.

Up and down they pumped their flukes as they propelled themselves through the sea. The cow and calf rose regularly to fill their lungs with air. Each time, they spouted misty fountains from their blowholes. Hour after hour the pair journeyed, under the sun and under the stars. Week after week, Humphrey and his mother swam through deep waters toward the Arctic.

The whales moved almost constantly. Around them everything else moved, too—the water, the passing ships, the creatures of the sea. The depths were home to dolphins, other kinds of whales, sea turtles, squid, and octopuses. Above the whales darted fish, **camouflaged** against the sunlight by their silvery bellies. Beneath the whales the dark backs of countless other fish blended with the blackness of the ocean depths. Far, far below, sunlight never reached. A seascape of mountains, valleys, and plains lay hidden, interrupted only by an occasional sunken ship.

When the water was calm, Humphrey and his mother traveled close to the surface. They stopped only to give the calf time to rest, nurse, and play. But, the ocean was not always peaceful.

One day, dark clouds gathered on the eastern horizon. The slow rise and fall of oceanic swells changed to choppy waves capped in white. The powerful waves tossed the surfacing whales. Lightning ripped the sky, and rain pelted down. Humphrey's mother led him far below where the water was calm. But storm or no storm, the whales needed air. Humphrey struggled upward and was knocked aside by a mountain of water. His mother steadied him with her body. He breathed quickly and again sought refuge underwater.

They fought the sea for hours. Gradually, the wind died, and the ocean regained its smooth roll. Sunlight

A storm at sea creates high, powerful waves that can be dangerous for whales when they rise to the surface to breathe. (Gloucester Fishermen's Museum)

broke through the clouds. The cow and calf passed the bloated body of a dead sperm whale. It was an old female lying belly up. Weakened by disease, she had been unable to survive the storm.

Alongside the lifeless whale, black fins cut the water—sharks! With their sharp teeth, they ripped out flesh and blubber. Humphrey and his mother fled.

A few weeks later, the cow and calf swam along-

A dead sperm whale floats on the sea's surface. Whales encounter storms and other dangers in the world's oceans. (William F. Dolphin)

side an abandoned fishing net. Nearly invisible, the net drifted at the surface. Caught inside it were dozens of fish—some rotting, some alive. The net extended more than fifty miles (eighty kilometers). As Humphrey and his mother traveled, they passed dead sea turtles and drowned birds. Near the far end of the net, two dolphins struggled to free themselves.

On and on the pair swam. Almost 3,000 miles

The cold Alaskan waters hold abundant food for hungry humpbacks such as Humphrey. (Cynthia D'Vincent/Ocean Research Under Sail)

(4,830 kilometers) from the breeding grounds, they reached their destination—the Arctic waters near Alaska.

The feeding grounds were not at all like the tropical environment of Humphrey's birth. Here, days were rarely sunny. Low-lying clouds concealed the snow-capped peaks of distant mountains. Rain drizzled almost every day. Underwater, the bays and passages teemed with food for hungry whales.

Humphrey and his mother entered a bay where fifty humpbacks fed. Around them the male and female adult whales hunted for food. Some were alone while others formed small or large pods. The competition of males for females was absent. This was the time for feeding, not mating.

Throughout the feeding season, Humphrey's mother helped him catch **prey**—tiny, shrimplike animals and fish. He skimmed the surface with his jaws apart. Close beside him and slightly ahead swam the cow. Into her calf's open mouth, she funneled prey. Unlike his mother's warm milk, the mouthfuls of food chilled Humphrey's insides.

All summer long, the humpbacks hunted. Sometimes Humphrey and his mother fed close to other cow-and-calf pairs. The young whale imitated his mother as she dove for food. But Humphrey could not capture all that he needed. He continued to nurse until he was a year old. By then, he was about thirty feet (nine meters) long—double his size at birth.

As summer turned to autumn, a few humpbacks sang. The whales began to leave the feeding grounds. Among the first to go were mature females with yearling calves, including Humphrey and his mother. By

In the feeding grounds, Humphrey and other males do not compete for females. Here, whales feed peacefully in groups. (Cynthia D'Vincent/ Ocean Research Under Sail)

December, all that were making the long trip to the breeding grounds had left. A few whales remained in Alaskan waters for the winter.

During Humphrey's second year in the feeding grounds, his mother was pregnant again. Although she left him alone, he stayed in the same area with her. Without difficulty, he caught enough food on his own.

The seasons and years passed. Humphrey grew

larger and stronger. Each fall he migrated south to the breeding grounds. Each spring he returned north. By the age of seven, Humphrey was sexually mature. In the tropics he competed with other males for the right to mate with females. By his tenth spring, the humpback was full grown. He weighed 38 tons (34.5 metric tons) and measured 40 feet (12.2 meters) in length. Like most adult males, Humphrey was slightly smaller than a mature female.

Migration Mysteries

No one has followed migrating humpbacks. It is not known whether the adults migrate alone or whether they meet other humpbacks. Scientists have many ideas, or theories, about migration. Yet, how these animals know when to begin, and how they find their way, remain mysteries.

In autumn several changes may trigger the humpbacks' southward migration. The number of prey has shrunk. The remaining prey are bigger. The sun does not rise as high as it had before. There are fewer hours of daylight, and the air is colder. Pregnant females near the time to give birth. Other adults feel an urge to mate.

After a winter in the breeding grounds, the humpbacks' blubber layer has slimmed. The resulting hunger may send the whales northward. Another signal may come from the increasing day length.

To find their way, humpbacks probably depend on methods used by other migrating animals. For part of their journey, they may use the sun and stars as maps. But the sky is often overcast. The humpbacks must orient themselves in other ways. They may sense the earth's **magnetic field**, and temperature and taste changes of the water. They may be guided by the sounds of ocean currents and of waves pounding shorelines many miles away. Or perhaps they follow underwater landmarks and retrace routes learned from their mothers.

Scientists have strong opinions for and against one theory. According to this theory, humpbacks "see" the ocean floor by using **echolocation**. They send out low frequency **sound waves**. The sound waves travel through the water, bounce off objects, and return as echoes. By listening to the echoes, the whales "see" what is beneath them. If this theory is correct, whales can use this method only near the coast. Farther out, the ocean floor is too deep.

Watery Highways

Humpbacks migrate through all the oceans of the world. To study their movements, scientists have organized information about individual whales. They have put together catalogs of photographs. The photographs identify humpbacks by their fluke and throat groove patterns. These markings identify individual humpbacks, just as fingerprints identify people. The catalogs also include information about where and when a particular humpback was seen. Scientists keep track of where whales are resighted. They have begun to map out migration routes.

Humphrey belongs to a population of about 2,700 humpbacks that lives in the North Pacific Ocean. These whales gather in Alaskan waters during the summer. In winter the population divides. Members migrate to breeding areas off the coasts of Mexico, Hawaii, and possibly Asia. Some may head for Hawaii one year and Mexico the next. Others may return to the same breeding ground year after year. Little is known about the humpbacks along the Asian coast. Whalemen killed so many that almost none are left.

Another 6,000 humpbacks live in the North Atlantic Ocean. Their feeding area includes the cold waters

Individual humpbacks can be identified by their fluke patterns. Five
different whales are shown in these six photographs. One whale is
shown twice, photographed in different years. Can you find it? (Ken-

neth C. Balcomb; Cynthia D'Vincent/Ocean Research Under Sail; Dr. Tom Ford, Jr.; Prudence Stuhr)

Asia

Europe

North Atlantic Ocean

Africa

South
America

Indian Ocean

South Atlantic Ocean

Antarctic Ocean

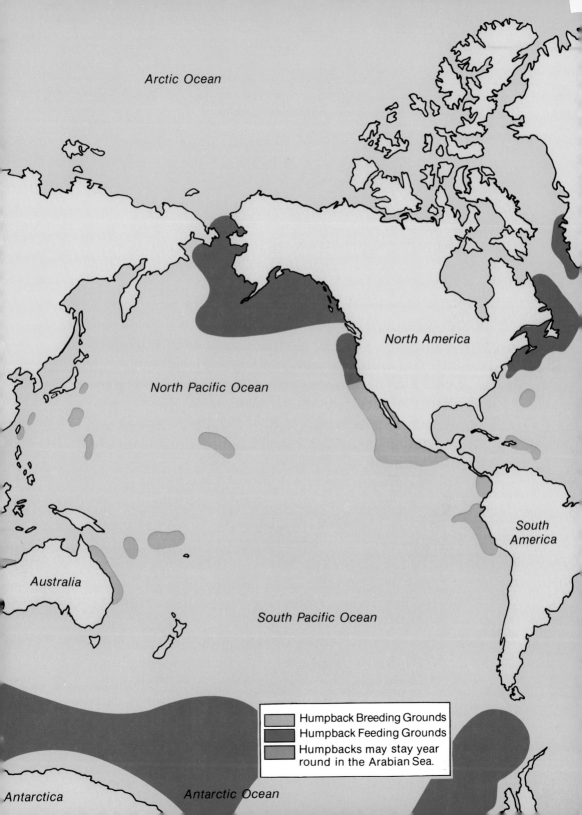

Arctic Ocean

North America

North Pacific Ocean

Australia

South Pacific Ocean

South America

Antarctica

Antarctic Ocean

Humpback Breeding Grounds
Humpback Feeding Grounds
Humpbacks may stay year round in the Arabian Sea.

from New England northward to Labrador and Greenland. These whales breed in the Caribbean and off the coast of Africa.

Scientists think small populations of humpbacks in the Arabian Sea and the northern Indian Ocean do not migrate. Food is plentiful year round in these regions. The water is warm enough for calving.

In the Southern Hemisphere, Antarctic waters provide plenty of food for whales. Another major population of humpbacks feeds in this cold, faraway region. These whales migrate to several breeding grounds near the equator.

The oceans of the Northern and Southern hemispheres are part of one huge world ocean. Yet, humpbacks from the two halves of the world do not meet. Both groups calve and breed near the equator, but at opposite times of the year. When summer comes to one of the poles, it is winter at the other.

In April and May, Antarctic whales leave the cold waters of the south polar feeding grounds and migrate toward the equator. At the same time, summer is coming for Northern Hemisphere humpbacks such as Humphrey. They begin the journey northward from the equator to the Arctic feeding grounds.

Humpbacks and fishermen sometimes compete for the same fish. (Cetacean Research Unit/Gloucester Fishermen's Museum)

A Whale of a Catch

Often humpbacks and fishermen share the feeding grounds, and they may compete for the same fish. Sometimes humpbacks become tangled up in long nets that are anchored to the ocean floor. If the whale cannot break free, it drowns. Off the eastern coasts of Canada and the United States as many as seventeen humpbacks have died in nets in a single year.

In the North Pacific Ocean, fishermen from Japan, South Korea, and Taiwan operate large ships. They remain at sea for months. When their nets break beyond repair, they toss them overboard. The discarded fish nets drift through the ocean. They continue to net fish and other marine animals. Humpbacks, however, don't appear to be part of the catch.

Keeping Warm and Keeping Cool

Humpbacks divide their time between frigid polar seas and warm tropical waters. They are adapted to the temperature extremes. Because they are mammals, their bodies maintain a constant temperature—about 97°F (36°C). The size of these creatures helps prevent their temperatures from dropping in cold water. A whale loses heat at its surface. Since its body has a small surface area in relation to its volume, the animal keeps much of its heat.

A humpback's behavior may help keep it warm, too. During sunny days on the Alaskan feeding grounds, the water at the surface may be 6°F (3.3°C) greater than its normal 48°F (9°C). Whales often bask in the sun. Their dark skin absorbs heat. On cold, cloudy days, humpbacks are more active. The heat generated by their muscles keeps them warm.

A humpback's blanket of blubber insulates, or shields, the great bulk of its body from cold. To reduce heat loss through blubberless fins, flukes, and flippers, blood flow to these areas is usually light. The flow of blood through them increases when a whale becomes overheated. The blood travels through tiny vessels called **capillaries** near the skin. From the capillaries, the unneeded heat escapes into the water, causing the whale to cool down.

While feeding, a humpback gulps gigantic mouthfuls of icy food and water. After swallowing, the animal has a bellyful of cold prey. Yet, no blubber insulates its insides. The whale is chilled, just as a person is when he or she drinks a glass of cold water.

When a whale dies, blood no longer flows through its body. Heat cannot escape. Yet, the blubber still insulates. As a result, if a whale is taken from the water shortly after death, its insides can actually cook. Bacteria produce heat and gases as they decompose, or break down, the body.

4 Table Manners

In the spring of 1985, Humphrey steamed into the chilly waters of Alaska. After six months with little to eat, the humpback was very hungry. He hunted a narrow ocean inlet, or fiord, with forty other whales. Near a fishing boat hidden by fog, Humphrey located a dense mass of **krill** and dived beneath the shrimp-like creatures. With his mouth open, he lunged upward through them. One-third of his body broke above the water line. Then with a thundering splash, he fell below the surface and closed his mouth.

Feeding alone, Humphrey ate whatever he could find. Sometimes it was krill, at other times fish. Later, he joined another whale, and the two hunted together. Humphrey and his partner breathed, dived, and lunged at the same time. Each of them caught more than they had on their own.

Circling gulls and swimming cormorants surrounded the surfacing whales. They grabbed fish and swooped away. A few birds plunged in and out of the

Two humpbacks breach together in the feeding grounds. (Cynthia D'Vincent/Ocean Research Under Sail)

Gulls swoop in for their share of the humpback's catch. (Cetacean Research Unit/Gloucester Fishermen's Museum)

humpbacks' open mouths. One moved too slowly. Humphrey swallowed it with the rest of his meal.

A trio of familiar humpbacks approached Humphrey and his companion. Two of them breached. They leapt high into the air, twisted around, and crashed back down. White foam sprayed around them. The whales grunted and groaned. When they quieted, all five fed together.

For a few hours, humpbacks alone and in groups joined and left Humphrey's pod. Some were known to Humphrey, while others were not. Later, the group broke up, and each whale followed its own course.

As days passed, the winds and currents changed. Tiny floating organisms were swept away, and the fish followed. Where Humphrey had been feeding, the food supply shrank. Now the same fiord supported only Humphrey and a few other humpbacks.

Humphrey again hunted with his companion. An unfamiliar humpback approached them. Humphrey and his partner breached again and again. Their blowholes above water, they let out high-pitched sounds called blats. The newcomer ignored the warning. Humphrey roared and bellowed. He charged, and smashed into the side of the unwanted whale. At this, the newcomer left. Humphrey and his companion scouted and fed together well into the night. Then, they parted.

Beneath a sea dimpled by light rain, Humphrey located herring. The ten-inch-long (twenty-six-centimeter long) fish swam in a loose school. Using bubbles, Humphrey rounded them up. He dove below the fish. From his blowholes, he released a cloud of small bubbles. The bubble cloud rose and expanded, driving

A humpback constructs a net of bubbles around its prey. With its mouth open, the whale swims up through the center of the net. (Cynthia D'Vincent/Ocean Research Under Sail)

thousands of the herring toward the water's surface. At the top, they had no escape. With his mouth open wide, Humphrey shot up through the bubbles and scooped up the fish.

In his endless search for food, Humphrey sometimes used another bubble technique. He spiraled below a mass of krill or fish and exhaled at intervals. At each spot where he breathed out, a column of air bubbles streamed upward. The columns formed a ring or "net" around the prey. The trapped animals fled from the bubbles toward the center of the net. To catch them, the humpback streaked up through the ring.

What's For Lunch?

The waters of the humpbacks' feeding grounds are cold, dense, and rich in nutrients. The nutrients support the plants and animals of the whales' **food chain**. At the base of the chain are tiny plants, such as diatoms and green algae. Through **photosynthesis**, these rootless plants capture and store the sun's energy. Suspended in open water, they grow only as deep as sunlight reaches.

Tiny animals graze on the floating plants. They, in turn, become the food of larger animals, including humpbacks. One type of small sea animals is krill. These **crustaceans** are about the length of your thumb. Rich in protein, they provide humpbacks with the nutrients needed for tissue growth and repair.

Krill swim packed in groups. Very dense schools may contain one million individuals per cubic yard of water. When abundant, krill color the sea red. In the Alaskan and Antarctic feeding grounds, they form the major part of the humpbacks' diet. In other areas, such as the North Atlantic feeding grounds, whales eat mainly small schooling fish. These include sand lance, herring, capelin, and other oily fish.

Fish move faster than krill. Yet, even in Alaskan waters, humpbacks hunt fish when they find them. Because of their high fat content, the oily fish are an excellent energy source. They provide more food energy per mouthful than a swallow of krill. In addition, the salt content of fish is lower than that of krill. Whales eating the tiny crustaceans must use energy to get rid of unneeded salt.

In a single day, a humpback consumes about a ton of food, often in a nonstop **feeding frenzy**. This is as much as a person eats in four years. The whale's body changes some of its food to blubber. During winter when the humpback eats little, it breaks down blubber for energy.

Pollution

The ocean has become a dumping ground for **toxic chemicals**. These poisons come from the production of plastics, medicines, and other useful products. Some chemicals are dumped directly into the sea by govern-

Many countries use the ocean as a dumping ground for toxic chemicals. (Greenpeace)

ments and industries. Others are poured into rivers that empty into the ocean.

Toxic chemicals used in farming enter the soil. Poisons seep from junk rotting in landfills. These poisons and chemicals from other sources wash out of the ground in the rain. They trickle into rivers and flow to the sea.

In the ocean, toxic chemicals are quickly taken up by plankton. Fish and krill eat the plankton, and the chemicals become part of their bodies. Whales, in turn, cannot avoid the poisons. Slowly, the amount of harmful chemicals builds up in their bodies. No one knows how these poisons affect humpbacks.

Some pollution, such as oil tanker spills, is accidental. On water, oil spreads into a thin layer. Much of it goes into the air or drifts to shore. Some is slowly broken down by bacteria and other tiny living things, while another part sinks to the ocean floor. The rest remains as floating lumps of tar.

Oil spills kill fish and destroy their breeding grounds. Some whale experts worry that whales may also suffer. Oil may kill their food supply and clog their baleen.

Kinds of Whales

Scientists separate whales into two groups according to whether or not they have teeth. One group, the **toothed whales**, includes sperm whales, killer whales, and dolphins. These animals capture large prey one at a time. The other group is the **baleen whales**. The largest animals ever to live on Earth, the blue whales,

A humpback fills its pouch with water and prey. It snaps its jaws shut. The baleen holds in the prey, and the water streams out. (Cynthia D'Vincent/Ocean Research Under Sail)

are baleen whales. So are the gray, fin, sei, minke, and right whales. The singers of the ocean, the humpbacks—including Humphrey—belong to this group, too.

Like all baleen whales, humpbacks have no teeth. Instead, they have long, thin **baleen plates**. From each side of their upper jaws, more than three hundred plates hang down like teeth on a comb. These plates are made of the same material as human fingernails. On the outer edges they are smooth. The inner edges split into a fringe of broomlike bristles that mesh together to form a filter.

When a humpback lunges mouth open through prey, gallons of food-filled water pour in. The tongue pushes downward, and the floor of the mouth opens. Long, parallel folds of skin under the whale's chin expand like a balloon. A pouch forms with the tongue as part of the back wall. Prey-filled water continues to rush in. When the pouch is full, the whale snaps its jaw shut.

The humpback holds its "lips" slightly apart. The tongue and the muscles around the pouch squeeze together. Water streams out between the baleen plates, trapping the food behind the mesh of bristles.

Baleen whales do not chew their food. Instead, they swallow it whole, and a set of three stomachs digests it.

Humpbacks can hold several hundred gallons of water in their pouches. Yet, these whales do not hunt fish much longer than twelve inches (thirty-one centimeters) because their throats are not suited to large prey.

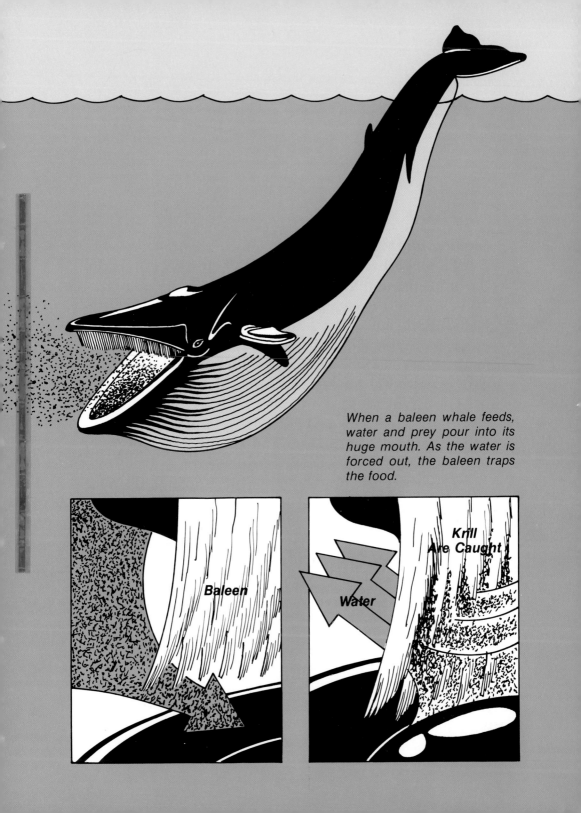

When a baleen whale feeds, water and prey pour into its huge mouth. As the water is forced out, the baleen traps the food.

Baleen

Water

Krill Are Caught

Feeding Methods

The feeding method a whale chooses depends on the kind and amount of prey available, the depth of the prey, and the ways a particular humpback prefers to feed. Bubble nets are made in J-shapes, U-shapes, and other circlelike shapes. Different kinds of lunging methods exist, too. Whales feeding near each other may or may not feed in the same manner.

Group feeding is common among humpbacks. Feeding can last for short periods—minutes or hours—and individual whales come and go. Other groups may feed together for entire seasons or years.

Whale experts observed one such pod made up of eight individuals. The pod was seen in Alaskan waters on various occasions during different years. When feeding on krill, the whales submerged. One member started to build a large bubble net about sixty-five feet (twenty meters) across. An underwater trumpetlike call was produced, and seven humpbacks rushed up together through the net. When it finished blowing bubbles, the first whale followed. The group repeated this action again and again. When feeding on herring, the pod dove underwater without making a bubble net. Just as before, the trumpeting sound was pro-

Scientists have observed members of this pod feeding together in different years. The scientists believe these whales use a trumpetlike call to organize their feeding. (Cynthia D'Vincent/Ocean Research Under Sail)

duced, and all eight whales lunged upward through the fish at the same time. Researchers believe that trumpeting was used to organize the whales.

Grunts, groans, and other social sounds are common in the feeding grounds. Scientists think that humpbacks use some sounds to alert others to a rich discovery of prey. Social sounds may also help humpbacks stay in contact when they cannot see each other.

5 A Whale of an Appetite

Ribbons of red streamed across the sky as the sun sank behind the horizon. The wind died. The waves quieted. Yet, the ocean surface did not grow calm. Scattered across a large Alaskan bay, Humphrey and thirty other humpbacks fed. They plunged in and out of the water. Scooping mouthful after mouthful of krill and sand lance, they gorged.

Nearby, tall fins zig-zagged swiftly across the bay. A pod of twenty killer whales shared the bounty with the humpbacks. Not disturbed by their presence, a humpback cow left her calf at the surface while she fed.

Twilight deepened into dusk. Having eaten his fill, Humphrey floated near the surface. Repeatedly, he poked his nostrils out of the sea, blew a high spout, and submerged. Other resting whales cruised through the water. In the muffled darkness of the night, humpbacks grazed and rested. Revving up at dawn, they began another feeding frenzy.

Seagulls perch on an iceberg during an Alaskan night. (William F. Dolphin)

By mid-morning, the food supply near the surface had disappeared. Humphrey rolled his head downward. He arched his back into the characteristic "hump" that gives his kind their common name. Lifting his flukes straight out of the water, he dove deep in search of prey. Down, down, down, to 400 feet (122 meters) below Humphrey zoomed. As he descended, the light decreased, and the pressure of the water surrounding him increased. Flickering shafts of sunlight outlined the creatures he passed, but their details remained hidden. Soon, Humphrey could barely make out the dusky shapes of nearby fish. Then, he was unable to see at all.

In the darkness, Humphrey heard the grunts, squeaks, and cracklings of fish. The noises of a moving school gave away its location. Humphrey chased the sounds, and gobbled down his quarry.

Twelve minutes after submerging, Humphrey completed his dive. Hissing like a steam engine, he surfaced and blew, surfaced and blew. He rid his body of stale air, and his lungs, blood, and muscles refilled with oxygen. Six minutes later, he dived deeply again.

As July passed into August, strong currents were formed by a summer storm. They carried away many

When preparing for a deep dive, a humpback arches its back into its characteristic "hump." (Cynthia D'Vincent/Ocean Research Under Sail)

When food is plentiful, killer whales and humpbacks eat together peacefully. (Dr. Tom Ford, Jr.)

of the tiny plants and animals in the humpbacks' food chain. For a short time, food became less abundant in Humphrey's range.

Humphrey had eaten more than seventy tons of food that summer. Yet, he was still driven to eat. As he hunted near a female humpback, the water carried threatening sounds. Twelve black fins sliced the water as a pack of hungry killer whales moved swiftly

*In times of danger, a humpback may slap the water with its flipper.
(Cynthia D'Vincent/Ocean Research Under Sail)*

toward the humpbacks. Sensing the danger, the cow slammed the water with her flipper. Humphrey slapped it with his tail.

The attackers neared. Turning her belly toward them, the cow lashed out with her flukes. Humphrey made loud wheezing blows and slapped the water with his flipper. The killer whales veered away. Quickly, they doubled back. Humphrey raised his chin

When threatened, Humphrey and other humpbacks may breach, thrusting their enormous bodies out of the water. (Cynthia D'Vincent/Ocean Research Under Sail)

and tail high out of the water. The female rolled over and thrashed her flukes. With its teeth, one of the attackers gashed the cow's tail. Humphrey breached again and again.

The killer whales circled in the distance and then left. Blood flowed from the cow's wound and darkened the water. With time, the injury would heal, but the humpback would bear the scar for life.

Feeding Frenzies

Abundant food near the surface triggers humpback feeding frenzies. With short, shallow dives, the whales hunt both krill and fish. In a flurry of activity, they spout and dive every two to four minutes.

Changes in light affect the number of prey at the surface. Krill, and some kinds of fish, move away from light. The tiny crustaceans spend the daylight hours in deep water. As the sun sets, they rise to the surface and graze under the protection of darkness. At sunrise, the krill retreat to the black depths. There, they remain hidden from predators that search by sight for food. When thick clouds block the sun, krill swim upward during the day. Then they get an extra meal.

When food is plentiful, humpbacks and killer whales feed side by side in peace. But when food is in short supply, a hungry pack of killer whales may attack humpbacks. Healthy humpbacks survive these encounters. Sick or very young ones may be torn apart.

Lack of food at the surface sends humpbacks deep underwater in search of prey. These deep, longer dives use more of a whale's energy than shallow dives and require more oxygen. Its lungs are more efficient than those of a human. In one breath, a person exchanges 15 percent of his or her air and fills the lungs half full. A humpback, however, exchanges 80 percent of its air and fills its lungs almost completely.

During deep dives, a humpback's heartbeat and other life-supporting processes slow. The whale's body shuts off blood flow to areas that are not vital. Oxygen is used very slowly. Blood and muscle cells release stored oxygen when it is required.

Competition for Food

Human populations are growing rapidly, and many countries depend more and more on the sea for food. In some areas of the world, fishermen compete with whales for fish. A few regions have already been overfished. There the humans—and whales—have had to look elsewhere for food.

Since krill are not tasty, few nations harvest them. However, the Russians use krill as food for both people and livestock. The Japanese catch krill, too. They feed the tiny crustaceans to fish in their fish farms.

In the future, hunger may force other countries to take advantage of krill. Because these crustaceans are a vital source of food for humpbacks, a major increase in krill catches could endanger the humpbacks.

Finding Prey

In the murky waters of the feeding grounds, humpbacks can see their food only at close range. At night, and at depths where little light reaches, this limited sight is useless.

To find their prey, humpbacks rely in part on their hearing. Their sense of touch may help, too. Single hairs stick out from the bumps on a humpback's jaws.

In the ocean, humpbacks rely on one or more of their senses to find their prey. (Cynthia D'Vincent/Ocean Research Under Sail)

Inside the skin, each hair connects to a nerve. Scientists think these hairs are sensitive to touch. The hairs may detect changes in water flow caused by moving animals, or they may sense only objects the whale actually touches.

Taste may also help in finding prey. Ocean animals are like "leaky bags," constantly taking in seawater and giving off waste materials. These wastes affect the taste of the water. According to some biologists, the wastes provide humpbacks with a flavored trail that may lead directly to a school of fish or krill. Other experts point out there is no evidence humpbacks can taste.

Smell plays little, if any, role in the humpbacks' hunt. Underwater, their blowholes stay closed, and odor-causing chemicals cannot be breathed. But even if they could be, humpbacks probably could not detect them. These whales have very small smelling centers in their brains.

Although they probably cannot sense it, some feeding humpbacks have "bad breath." Their spouts smell like a ton of rotten fish. There are probably many different causes of bad breath in whales. However, a Boston dentist with an interest in whales discovered the source in at least one humpback. The whale's spout carried bacteria from the air passages similar to the bacteria that cause the disease **diphtheria** in humans and other animals. One effect of diphtheria bacteria is to inflame the upper air passages. As a result, the body produces foul-smelling breath. Fortunately for whale watchers and scientists, humpback diphtheria is not a threat to humans.

Wrong-way Humphrey

As summer faded into autumn, humpbacks migrated from the chilly waters of Alaska. Like his parents, grandparents, and countless other humpbacks before him, Humphrey obeyed an inner drive. He journeyed past the coasts of Washington and Oregon. After days and nights of travel, he entered California waters.

Thirty miles (forty-eight kilometers) west of San Francisco, Humphrey stopped to feed near the Farallon Islands. He did not continue in toward the breeding grounds. Instead, he strayed toward San Francisco Bay. Propelled by his powerful flukes, he fought the tidal currents that rushed between the bay and the Pacific Ocean. Humphrey slipped beneath the Golden Gate Bridge. Cars and trucks thundered above him. Waves crashed against the rocky shores of the narrow channel. Shielded by darkness, Humphrey swam unnoticed past freighters, pleasure craft, and fishing boats.

On October 11, 1985, Californians spotted Humphrey inside San Francisco Bay. On that day the part of his life we know about began. Crowds stared at him. Children cheered. Scientists and television crews recorded his movements.

For several days, Humphrey toured the bay. Surfacing regularly to spout, the humpback cruised by Oakland and the harbor islands. While swimming past the Berkeley Marina, he ran aground in shallow water. His exposed skin, dark and healthy, glistened in the sun. Back and forth, up and down, Humphrey waved his flukes. He freed himself and plunged into deeper water.

Coast Guard officials and biologists from the California Marine Mammal Center became concerned for the whale's well-being. With boats, they tried to herd the humpback out to sea. Humphrey had no understanding of their purpose. Dodging the small vessels, he traveled northward toward the Sacramento River Delta.

The farther from the ocean the whale journeyed, the less salty his watery environment became. In the delta, the water was almost completely salt free. Being less dense, the fresh water did not hold Humphrey up as well as salt water. As a result, the whale required more energy to swim, dive, and surface.

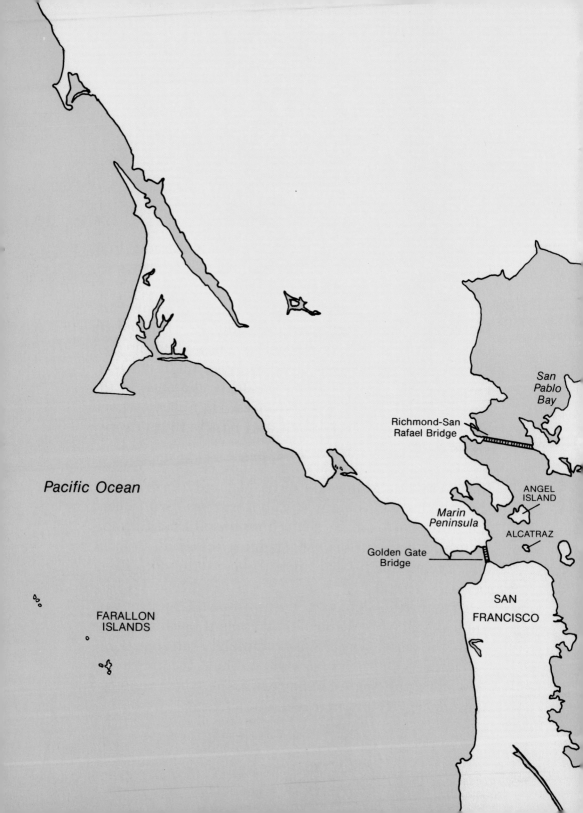

Pacific Ocean

San
Pablo
Bay

Richmond-San
Rafael Bridge

ANGEL
ISLAND

Marin
Peninsula

ALCATRAZ

Golden Gate
Bridge

SAN
FRANCISCO

FARALLON
ISLANDS

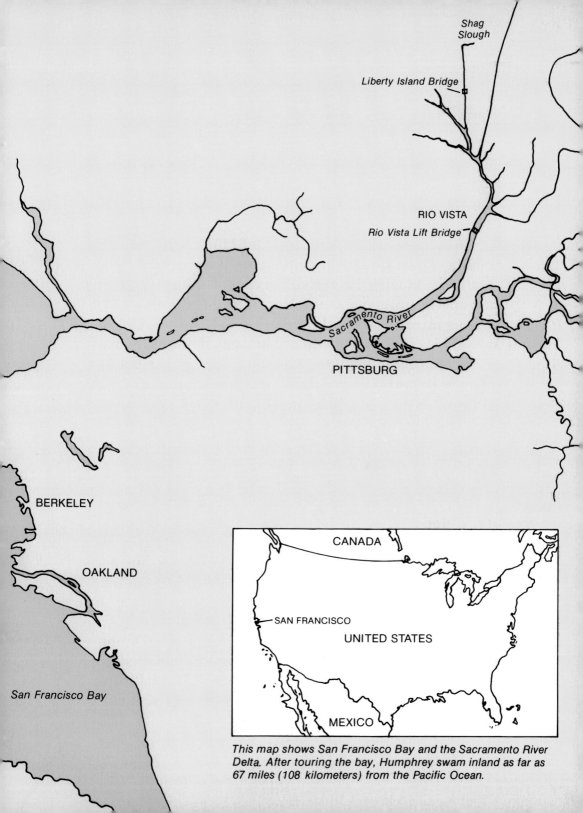

Shag
Slough

Liberty Island Bridge

RIO VISTA
Rio Vista Lift Bridge

Sacramento River

PITTSBURG

BERKELEY

OAKLAND

San Francisco Bay

CANADA

SAN FRANCISCO

UNITED STATES

MEXICO

This map shows San Francisco Bay and the Sacramento River Delta. After touring the bay, Humphrey swam inland as far as 67 miles (108 kilometers) from the Pacific Ocean.

Rescue workers kept track of Humphrey's movements. They stayed in contact with agents from the National Marine Fisheries Service. This government agency approved each action taken throughout the rescue effort.

By Day Five of his inland journey, Humphrey had wandered 50 miles (80.5 kilometers) from the Pacific Ocean. Experts, worried that the lost whale could not find his way back, tried again to reverse his direction. Rescue workers used underwater speakers. Upstream from the humpback, they broadcast the noises of killer whales. Downstream, they played tapes of common humpback social sounds.

The speakers were not powerful enough to cause Humphrey to swim downstream. Instead, he swam farther inland and became stranded on a sandbar. For several hours, Humphrey waved his flukes up and down, back and forth. His efforts were in vain. His back remained above water, and the sun burned his exposed skin.

By chance, a large barge neared the beached humpback and panicked him. As whale-lovers on shore chanted "Go, whale, go!" Humphrey lunged three times, lashed his tail, and dove into deeper water.

Unknowingly, the humpback played a game of cat-and-mouse. When the crews of four patrol boats and a rubber raft tried to block his upstream movements, he escaped them. The next day, Humphrey swam toward the Rio Vista lift bridge. Above him, work crews repaired the bridge. Despite the banging and hammering, Humphrey streaked beneath the structure and continued upstream.

On Day Seven, officials again tried to corral Humphrey with boats. A Coast Guard helicopter circled noisily overhead. This up-in-the-air approach to herding had been successful with humpbacks elsewhere. With Humphrey, it failed.

Discouraged officials changed their plan of action. At the suggestion of a concerned citizen, they played classical music to coax the whale. It seemed to work — Humphrey headed downstream. But when the whale reached the Rio Vista Bridge, he made a U-turn and swam back the other way.

For days, Humphrey swam south, and Humphrey swam north. He stayed on the upstream side of the lift bridge. Even though officials closed the bridge to traffic, the whale would not go under it. Instead, on Day Eight, Humphrey passed beneath another bridge far-

On Day Eight of his inland journey, Humphrey swam under the Liberty Island Bridge. (Bob Wilson/California Marine Mammal Center)

ther north—the Liberty Island Bridge. On Day Ten, he entered Shag Slough, a shallow, dead-end backwater polluted by poisonous crop sprays from nearby fields.

For five days, Humphrey remained in the narrow slough, 67 miles (108 kilometers) from the ocean. The forty-foot (twelve-meter) whale had barely enough room to swim in a circle. He breathed irregularly, and his blows weakened. The fresh water flushed out his body salts. His black skin lightened to gray and bloated, and bits of his water-logged hide peeled off. Biologists worried that soon sensitive underlying tissues would be exposed and damaged. Whale watchers on shore felt they were keeping a death watch.

Lost in Fresh Water

No one knows why Humphrey strayed so far from the ocean. When he first entered San Francisco Bay, observers worried that he was ill and had no sense of his location. Some wondered if he was suffering from the effects of **parasites**. Barnacles and whale lice are parasites that live on the skin of humpbacks. They pose no threat to the whales' health. Some types of parasitic worms may invade inner regions such as the blubber, liver, or intestines. They are not known to cause strange behavior. **Brain flukes**, on the other hand, are deadly wormlike parasites. They enter whales and dolphins through the ears, travel to the brain, and cause the animal to lose its sense of direction and die. The presence of brain flukes in humpbacks has never been documented.

In the beginning, biologists saw no signs of illness in Humphrey. He swam with strong strokes of his tail

While Humphrey stayed in Shag Slough, whale watchers could observe the scars on Humphrey's fin. (Bob Wilson/California Marine Mammal Center)

and flippers and breathed regularly. His skin appeared dark and healthy.

Disease was ruled out. Some people thought that Humphrey was a pregnant cow. They reasoned that if the whale was ready to give birth, "she" might be searching for warm, sheltered waters.

Since the delta waters were not clear enough to see through, divers did not attempt to swim under the humpback to determine its sex. Yet, experts from the California Marine Mammal Center were reasonably certain Humphrey was male. They pointed out that scars on Humphrey's fin were similar to scars on fins of known males. On the other whales, the scars had resulted from fights over females. The scientists believed that Humphrey had fought during his winters on the breeding grounds. In addition, humpbacks in the North Pacific Ocean usually give birth between January and March. This was October. Finally, no records tell of a humpback bearing young in fresh water.

A Vanishing Breed

Whales are concealed by water most of the time and they travel great distances. As a result, it is difficult to make an exact count of their population. Scientists estimate that there are only 15,000 to 20,000 humpbacks worldwide. Because the killing of whales has greatly reduced the number of humpbacks, these giant mammals are in danger of vanishing from the earth.

Humphrey is a member of an **endangered species**. He is protected by the Marine Mammal Protection Act

Many people made a special trip to see Wrong-way Humphrey. (Bob Wilson/California Marine Mammal Center)

and the Endangered Species Act. These laws make it a crime to go near humpbacks and other endangered species, except by special permit. The National Marine Fisheries Service enforces both of these laws. When Humphrey detoured into San Francisco Bay, it was the job of this agency to take charge.

Officials of the National Marine Fisheries Service worked with local, state, and federal law enforcement agencies, as well as whale experts and 150 volunteers from the California Marine Mammal Center. They also worked with other scientists and elected officials. The rescue team had the task of returning Humphrey to the ocean. In addition, they had to protect him from people who could hurt him—by accident or on purpose.

Public Concern Over Humphrey

Thousands of people responded to Humphrey's plight. Eager to glimpse the wayward whale, spectators jammed the banks and bridges of the Sacramento Delta. Overhead, reporters in helicopters worked to update the nation on the humpback's progress.

At first the whale did not have a name. Some people called him E.T. because they thought he was far from home, but the name did not catch on. The operators of a Rio Vista restaurant came up with another name—Humphrey. They thought it sounded right for a humpback. To honor the visiting whale, they created a special dish—"Swordfish a la Humphrey." Hungry whale watchers liked both the dish and the name.

While Humphrey centered his stay near Rio Vista, the town became an instant tourist center. Business at restaurants and gas stations boomed. Fast-thinking entrepreneurs sold T-shirts with messages such as "Have a whale of a time," and "Humphrey Vacationed at Rio Vista, California."

Upset by the lack of progress, whale lovers offered their own suggestions for rescuing Humphrey. On the lighter side was a list of tips gleaned from thousands of calls to the California Marine Mammal Center:

● The Salt Solution: Make a trail with salt cubes, and the whale will follow it to the ocean.

● The Roundup: Get a noisy helicopter and attach half a dead cow to it. Dangle the body in the water. The hungry whale will try to catch the beef.

● The Holdup: Put a harness around the 38-ton (34.5-metric-ton) animal. Lift him from the water by helicopter, lower him onto a barge, and float him out to sea.

● The Mating Game: Drop a female humpback into the delta and let the pair swim out together.

● The Modern Art Technique: Using papier mâché, build an enormous female humpback. Drag it in front of the whale to attract him away from the delta.

7 The Great Whale Rescue

On Day Fifteen, Humphrey remained, still self-imprisoned, in Shag Slough. The rescue workers tried a new plan to free him. They filled ten sections of pipe with water. Six small boats, with the pipes aboard, formed a horseshoe behind the whale. Using ropes, crew members positioned the pipes so that part of their length was underwater. Above the water line, they banged on them with metal hammers.

Underwater, the pipes chimed in low tones, creating a curtain of sound. Chased by the chimes, Humphrey slowly retreated downstream. At the Liberty Island Bridge he stopped.

Again and again, the boats closed in. Each time, Humphrey swam toward the bridge and then veered away and spouted with a stressed screech.

Workers used special equipment to scan beneath the bridge. They discovered broken pilings from an older bridge that stuck up several feet from the bottom of the river. In places, the water was only twelve feet

In an attempt to move Humphrey downstream toward the ocean, workers slung water-filled pipes over the side of boats and banged on them. (Bob Wilson/California Marine Mammal Center)

(less than four meters) deep. Humphrey was about the same from back to belly. In addition, the space between the existing pilings was less than the span of his two long flippers.

The humpback had slipped past both the old and new pilings on his way *into* the slough, but now they kept him from leaving. To give the whale more space, workers cleaned under the bridge. The next day, the rescue boats again surrounded Humphrey on three sides. The volunteers slung pipes overboard, and banged gently.

Humphrey edged toward the Liberty Island Bridge. He rolled on his side and crashed his giant flipper against the surface. Water sprayed into the air.

When the boats retreated, the whale quieted. Then the rescuers advanced again, banging the pipes. The disturbed humpback neared the structure once more and tried to pass under it. Twice he became stuck on a sandbar by the bridge. Twice he broke free.

As the afternoon went on, the weary rescue team wondered if they would ever succeed. Officials from the National Marine Fisheries Service stopped the drive. After forty-five minutes, the rescue team made one last try. The boats advanced until they were almost on top of Humphrey. Without a pause, the workers on board banged louder than they had before.

The whale was surrounded. He had no place to go, except toward the people or under the bridge. Suddenly, he shot beneath the structure but turned before clearing it. His head wedged between columns in one piling, and his flukes and flippers jammed in a neighboring piling.

As boats chased Humphrey toward the Liberty Island Bridge, rescue workers on top of the bridge prepared a net. They planned to throw it down after the whale passed under the bridge. (Bob Wilson/California Marine Mammal Center (top), and the San Francisco Examiner)

Humphrey panicked. He wheezed and thrust his head above water. Back and forth he thrashed. The bridge shook. At last the humpback made a great heaving sound. Rolling his body from side to side, he broke free. Humphrey squeezed through the Liberty Island Bridge and zoomed downstream. At nightfall, his human followers lost track of him near the Rio Vista lift bridge.

By dawn of Day Sixteen, Humphrey returned to the Liberty Island Bridge. A farmer who lived near the bridge spotted the whale. He found a pipe left by a rescue worker and rushed to the water. Quickly, he plunged the pipe into the water and struck it with a hammer. Humphrey turned around and headed back to the lift bridge. As if confused, he twice passed back and forth beneath it. Finally, he swam under the Rio Vista Bridge and continued downstream.

Humphrey lingered in the backwaters of the Sacramento River Delta, 60 miles (96.6 kilometers) from his natural environment. Escorted by a fleet of boats, he swam downstream during the day. Under cover of darkness, he backtracked to the nearest bridge or other barrier. The National Marine Fisheries Service wanted to keep track of Humphrey's nighttime wanderings. They decided to place on the whale a small **radio tag** that sent out electronic signals.

On Day Seventeen, using a 15-foot (4.6-meter) pole, a scientist lowered a cylinder-shaped tag with a suction cup onto Humphrey. The tag fell off, and another kind was tried. With a special gun, a small radio tag was fired into Humphrey's skin. This tag fell off, too. On Day Twenty-three, a government scientist tried a third kind of tag. Armed with a crossbow, he shot the tag into Humphrey. It lodged close to the whale's fin. This human triumph was short-lived. The tag held for only a day.

The longer Humphrey stayed in fresh water, the more his skin peeled. Blisters formed, and his eyes and breathing passages became more irritated.

Whale experts from Canada and the United States talked by telephone for three hours. They debated whether to leave Humphrey alone or to try other rescue methods. Most feared he would soon be too weak to return to the ocean. The experts came up with a new plan to save Humphrey from himself.

Early on Day Twenty-four, more than fifty Navy, Coast Guard, Army, sheriff department, and privately owned vessels formed a fleet on the Sacramento Delta.

A fleet of boats herds Humphrey toward San Francisco Bay and the Pacific Ocean. (Bob Wilson/California Marine Mammal Center)

On board, 500 rescue workers prepared to herd Humphrey with a wide barrier of chimes.

One boat, the *Bootlegger*, positioned itself in front of Humphrey. Crew members readied underwater speakers. They planned to broadcast recorded sounds of a pod of humpbacks. The sounds included the unusual trumpeting call produced during special feeding situations.

A signal was given, the tapes rolled, and Humphrey spun southward. Down the delta, he chased the *Bootlegger*. Humphrey was urged on by the chimes, the trumpeting calls, and sometimes no sounds at all. In seven hours he moved more than 40 miles (64.4 kilometers) downstream. At times, the whale swam beside the boat. By the end of the day, he spouted within 4 miles (6.4 kilometers) of the Golden Gate Bridge.

As usual, Humphrey escaped the rescue workers during the night. The next day, they found him 6 miles (9.7 kilometers) farther from the ocean. Officials replayed the feeding tapes, but the whale did not follow. Instead, as whale-watchers gathered, Humphrey swam in circles. He slammed his flippers and flukes against the water, creating fountains of spray. He lunged above the surface, breached almost straight out of the water, then kerplopped with a splash.

Finishing his show, Humphrey seemed to nap. When he awoke, crew members on Navy patrol boats banged pipes. Once more, the crew of the lead boat played the feeding sounds. Humphrey moved toward the Pacific again. Back in San Francisco Bay, he detoured around Angel Island. He visited Alcatraz and paused near the San Francisco waterfront.

On his way back to the ocean, Humphrey swam past Alcatraz Island in San Francisco Bay. (California Office of Tourism)

Late in the day, Humphrey followed the *Bootlegger* toward the Golden Gate Bridge. As his fans cheered, the celebrated whale spouted twice and slipped beneath the fog-enshrouded bridge. Home at last, Humphrey the wrong-way whale disappeared from view.

Whale experts hoped to glimpse Humphrey again— bubble-feeding, singing, or fighting. They wanted to know if the humpback had survived. Some joked that he had enjoyed his inland journey so much he would someday lead 150 whales into San Francisco Bay.

Humphrey's fluke markings had been photographed. Many people learned about the markings through a bulletin of the California Marine Mammal Center. Scientists waited for the whale to turn up, and on August 16, 1986, their wish came true. Humphrey was sited with a companion 30 miles (48.3 kilometers) west of San Francisco. The pair swam near the Farallon Islands along with about seventy-five other humpbacks and sixty blue whales.

Protecting Humpback Habitats

Scientists are studying the whales that visit the Farallon Islands. In recent summers, humpbacks have

Humphrey's fluke markings identify him in the same way that finger-prints identify people. (Kenneth C. Balcomb)

been observed feeding there. These islands may be part of Humphrey's feeding grounds.

The Farallon Islands are in a national marine sanctuary. The sanctuary, which includes the ocean around the islands and part of the California coast, was set up to preserve and protect the marine environment. Efforts have been made to create sanctuaries in Hawaiian and Alaskan waters. Whale experts want

Whale research ships such as this one in Alaskan waters help scientists learn more about humpbacks and their habitat. (Cynthia D'Vincent/ Ocean Research Under Sail)

the humpbacks' habitat protected at both ends of its migratory route.

Humphrey's Legacy

In the weeks and months following Humphrey's inland adventure, the expenses from the rescue effort were added up. The total came to $90,000. The state and federal governments paid $55,000. The California

Marine Mammal Center raised the remaining $35,000 through private donations.

Some people believed the money was misspent. They pointed out that many marine biologists have difficulty getting funds for whale research. The money used to rescue Humphrey could have supported several years of study. These critics thought that if Humphrey had been left alone from the start, he might have reached the ocean without help.

A few scientists questioned the value of rescuing a confused whale. They pointed out that Humphrey may now breed and could produce offspring that also migrate improperly. They argued that all humpbacks benefit when whales like Humphrey do *not* reproduce.

Owners of river front property in the Sacramento River Delta complained of damage caused by trespassing whale watchers. Public property was affected, too. At the Antioch Dunes Federal Wildlife Refuge, Humphrey fans trampled rare plants.

Still, many people felt the effort and money spent on Humphrey were worthwhile. His inland journey provided biologists with new insights. As expected, the whale's skin began to break down after a week in fresh water. Humphrey showed, however, that humpbacks can survive this condition longer than experts had thought.

Humphrey's travels appeared to relate to the direction of tides and currents. Repeatedly, the whale swam *against* the current. He moved downstream as the tide came in and upstream as the tide went out.

News of the strange journey sparked the nation's interest. As people learned of one whale's plight, they grew concerned for all whales. Humphrey came to stand for the recent change in thinking about the hunting of whales. A blubber processing plant was once located in Richmond, gateway to the Sacramento Delta. The plant, which was one of the last traces of the American whaling industry, was closed in the 1950s. Before then, a fleet of boats pursued a whale to kill it. In 1985, another fleet formed to save one.

8 A Close Call for Humpbacks

Today, throughout the world, many people and organizations are working hard to save humpbacks and other whales. Why should anyone care about protecting these magnificent mammals? What difference would it make if they disappeared forever? A turn-of-the-century naturalist, William Beebe, put it this way: "When the last individual of a race of living things breathes no more, another heaven and another earth must pass before such a one can be again. . ."

Many people say that the **extinction** of one kind of animal or plant is unfortunate, but not an event of great concern. If the effect could be limited to just one animal, this might be a reasonable point of view. Life on earth, however, does not work that way. Each kind of animal and plant has adapted itself to live with others in its environment. When one form of life disappears, others are affected. Whenever people cause the destruction of a **species**, another link in Earth's community of life is lost.

Water streams from a humpback's tail flukes at night. (Cynthia D'Vincent/ Ocean Research Under Sail)

Today the world's plants and animals are disappearing at an alarming rate. If people do not act to save the humpbacks and other whales, we will have failed to preserve one of the important links in the global community of life. We may not realize until they are gone that these animals are vital to life as we know it.

Plants and animals provide us with food and medicines and many other valuable materials. Without them, humans could not live for long on earth. Yet in the past, throughout the world's oceans, people have hunted the humpbacks and other whales almost to extinction.

Whales have been important to humans at least since the Stone Age. At the start, people used nearly the entire whale body. They ate the meat and turned other parts into objects they needed. Baleen became sled runners, archer's bows, and knife handles. From the heavy bones, people built fences and chairs, clubs and axes. For centuries before electricity, natural gas, and petroleum came into use, whale oil provided the best lighting.

Yankee Whaling

When the Pilgrims sailed into Cape Cod Bay in 1620, they noticed large numbers of whales and recognized their commercial value. During the early years of the colony, settlers harvested only the whales found on the beach. Soon, colonists built small whaling boats and hired Indian whalemen to help them hunt whales offshore. **Cutting-in** and **trying-out**—cutting and boiling strips of blubber to obtain whale oil—were done on the beach.

Norwegian cave drawings such as this one are among the earliest records of the importance of whales. Some are 4,000 years old. (University Museum of National Antiquities, Oslo, Norway)

In the early 1700s, the island of Nantucket, off the Massachusetts coast, became the world's leading whaling port. Nantucket whalemen built larger boats than the earlier settlers. They first hunted right whales, so named because they were easy to catch. These creatures lived close to shore and swam slower than other whales. They floated when dead, making them much easier to tow than humpbacks, which sank.

Gradually, whales became scarce in the waters around Nantucket and along other coasts where hunting was heavy. New England whalemen had to sail farther in search of whales.

Early in the eighteenth century, a Nantucket whaling ship was blown far out to sea during a storm. In deep ocean waters, great herds of sperm whales were discovered. The oil of these animals was of higher quality than that of right whales.

Whale hunters were eager to profit from the valuable sperm whales. To capture them in their deep ocean habitat, Yankee whalemen built large sailing vessels that carried smaller whaleboats. Since the ships traveled vast distances from shore, **tryworks**—brick furnaces used to boil strips of blubber—were constructed on deck. The all-male crews roamed the world. In nearly every ocean, whalemen found and slaughtered sperm and right whales. They also killed a smaller number of humpbacks and other whales. After two to four years at sea, the ships returned home, sometimes with their holds full.

On both sides of the Atlantic Ocean, towns and cities expanded. The need for whale products grew. The oil from humpbacks and other baleen whales was

The Yankee whaling ship, Greyhound, *in full sail. (The Whaling Museum, New Bedford, Mass.)*

used for lamp fuel, and for making wool cloth and soap. The baleen plates—stiff, yet flexible—were molded into the ribs of umbrellas and corsets. Shredded, they became watch springs and chair stuffing.

To meet the demand, American and British whalemen killed thousands and thousands of whales. Yankee whaling peaked during the mid-nineteenth century. New Bedford, Massachusetts, was the busiest whaling port in America, and most people in the town earned their living from whaling. Thousands were employed making casks, ropes, **harpoons**, and other items needed on whaling ships. Others refined oil for lighting and machine lubricants. Some made candles.

In 1859, the discovery of petroleum in Pennsylvania led to a decline in the whaling industry. Many products were produced from this dark liquid, including a lighting fluid called kerosene. Kerosene burned brighter than whale oil and was cheaper. Paraffin wax, another petroleum product, was used to make candles. As petroleum products replaced whale products, the demand for and price of whale and sperm oils began to drop. The American whaling industry declined, but it did not die completely.

Yankee whaling succeeded at a price. Throughout

The New Bedford, Massachusetts, waterfront bustled with activity during the time of Yankee whaling. (The Kendall Whaling Museum, Sharon, Mass.)

the world, sperm whales and right whales dropped in number. Yet, few whalemen cared about the harm they did to whale populations. They believed these creatures of the sea existed to serve humankind.

During the height of Yankee whaling, many humpbacks were killed in the North Atlantic Ocean. Humpbacks were taken from other oceans, too. However, for humpbacks, the hunt had barely begun.

Modern Whaling

Before modern whaling began, humpbacks and other baleen whales were hunted only in shallow water. Men in sailing ships could not catch these fast-moving animals in the open ocean. By the mid-1800s, the number of sperm and right whales had greatly decreased. Svend Foyn, a Norwegian, realized that the lack of prey could doom the whaling industry. Foyn found a way to save it. Using steam boats, harpoon guns, and compressed air, he and other Norwegians developed a new way to hunt whales. Their methods changed the whaling industry. Whalemen could now kill large, fast-moving whales that sank just as easily as slow-moving whales that didn't sink.

Along their own coast, the Norwegians used the new methods. They towed the dead whales to shore to be butchered. The shore stations used motorized winches and saws. Workers processed many more whales than was possible using hand tools on sail-powered whaling ships.

Later, to meet the demand for whale products, the Norwegians set up shore factories in many parts of the world. Other nations modernized and built shore stations, too. Tens of thousands of whales were killed.

A dead baleen whale moves on a slipway to a modern shore station. (Greenpeace)

Humpbacks made easy targets for modern whalemen. In many places, these whales fed and bred close to shore. They swam slower than other large baleen whales, and approached boats instead of fleeing from them. Yet, no whale anywhere in the world was safe from attack. Blue, fin, sei, minke, gray, and sperm whales were also killed.

The United States took part in shore whaling

along the Pacific coast. About 1850, the first shore station was built. From Alaska to Mexico, migrating gray whales and humpbacks were hunted. Perhaps some of these were Humphrey's ancestors. At first, traditional whaling methods were used, but in 1905, the shore whalemen switched to modern methods. After many of the whales along the Pacific coast were killed, most of the shore stations closed. The Japanese hunted humpbacks on the other side of the ocean. As a result, the North Pacific humpback population was nearly wiped out.

Whales soon disappeared from the old whaling grounds, but still the whalemen did not quit. They discovered a new place to hunt whales. The cold oceans near Antarctica teemed with baleen whales.

The first shore station to serve the Antarctic whalemen was built on an island off the tip of South America. Other stations were soon built on neighboring islands. During the early twentieth century, thousands of humpbacks and other whales were killed near Antarctica. Each shore station processed as many as thirty whales a day.

Modern European whaling thrived. The invention of **hydrogenation** provided a new market for whale oil.

A huge Japanese factory ship cruises the oceans in search of whales. (Greenpeace)

The process of hydrogenation changed liquid whale oil into a solid, odorless fat. In solid form, the oil was used in making soap and margarine. Large amounts of money were made in this new market.

The invention of electric refrigerators and freezers provided another new market for whale products. The machines made it possible for whale meat to be frozen and shipped far from the whaling grounds. The Japanese used large amounts of this beeflike meat for food.

In the period before World War II, whaling companies built floating factory ships. The British, Norwegians, and Germans sent the most ships into the Antarctic region. Soon, floating factories cruised all the oceans of the world. Wherever enough whales lived, mother ships sent motorized **chaser boats** to harvest them.

Saving the Whales

In 1931 and 1937, some countries with whaling fleets signed agreements in an attempt to establish rules for Antarctic whaling. These agreements did not succeed in protecting humpbacks because most whaling nations did not sign or observe them. Whaling increased until World War II. Then it came almost to a standstill, and whale populations began to recover.

After the war, the demand for animal fats used in food products rose in western nations. In search of new markets and larger profits, some countries improved whaling methods and killed more whales. Japan, Norway, Great Britain, the Soviet Union, and the Netherlands had the largest whaling fleets.

Soon after the war ended, the International Whaling Commission was established. It is made up of most nations involved in whaling, and some that are not. Its job is to make rules that will help preserve whales in all the world's oceans. The commission allowed a limited number of humpbacks to be killed in the Antarctic Ocean, but humpback whaling in other places was not affected.

In 1963, the hunting of humpbacks in the Southern Hemisphere was stopped completely. Three years later, with a few exceptions, humpbacks were protected worldwide. Then, in 1985, the hunting of humpbacks was totally banned. Some whale experts fear that a few humpbacks are still being killed.

Global concern for humpbacks saved them from extinction during the twentieth century. The killing has stopped, but humpback songs may still be silenced. These whales are not yet safe. Pollution, fishing nets, and human competition for their food are serious threats. To make sure Humphrey and his children survive, we must protect their habitat. Humankind must find a way to use the oceans without destroying the creatures that inhabit them.

Appendix A:
Learning More About
Humpback Whales

The following activities will help you learn more about whales.

1. Go on a whale watch. If you live near the sea, or visit a coastal area, take a whale-watching cruise. This special boat ride will give you the chance to view whales in the wild. You may be able to see whales spout, dive, and feed. Most whale watches are led by experts. They will point out the whales and identify them for you.

2. Listen to the songs of humpback whales. Many libraries have recordings of singing humpbacks. Ask your librarian to help you find a record or tape of humpback songs.

3. Visit a whaling museum. A visit to a whaling museum can transport you back to the time of Yankee whaling. The Mystic Seaport Museum is located in Mystic, Connecticut. There, you can climb aboard the *Charles W. Morgan*, the last of the Yankee wooden whaling ships, and see how whale hunters worked and lived. The Whaling Museum in New Bedford, Massachusetts, has a half-size, model of a whaling ship that you can explore. The collection at the Kendall Whaling Museum in Sharon, Massachusetts, includes paintings, old whaling weapons, and much more.

4. Learn about efforts to rescue sick or injured marine mammals and to preserve and protect those that are endangered. The California Marine Mammal Center rescues sick and injured seals, sea lions, dolphins, and whales that strand, or run aground, along the California coast. The center is a private, nonprofit agency located in the Marin Headlands, just north of the Golden Gate Bridge. You can visit free of charge every day of the year and see how the staff cares for seals and sea lions. (Whales and dolphins are cared for elsewhere.) When the animals are healthy again, they are returned to the ocean. The hospital is run with a 95 percent volunteer staff. For further information contact the California Marine Mammal Center, Marin Headlands, Fort Cronkite, California, 94965. Phone: (415) 331-SEAL.

The Pacific Whale Foundation, located in Kihei on the island of Maui, Hawaii, works to preserve and protect endangered marine mammals. The nonprofit foundation carries out research, conservation, and education programs involving whales, dolphins, porpoises, and other marine mammals. Currently it is studying the effects of increased human activity in the humpback's Hawaiian breeding grounds.

Appendix B:
Scientific Names for
Sea Animals

Sea creatures, like all living things, have two kinds of names. The first is their *common name*, a name in the everyday language of an area where they are found. An animal often has a number of different common names in different languages. Also, several different animals may be known by the same common name.

The second kind of name is their *scientific name*. This is a Latin name assigned by scientists to identify an animal all over the world for other scientists. The scientific name is usually made up of two words. The first identifies the genus, or group, of similar animals (or plants), and the second identifies the species, or kind, of animal in the group. Sometimes, as scientists learn more about an animal, they may decide it belongs in a different group. The scientific name is then changed so that all scientists can recognize it and know exactly what animal it refers to.

If you want to learn more about the creatures in this book, the list of scientific names that follows will be useful to you. A typical species has been identified for each type of animal mentioned in the book. There may be many other species in the same group.

Chapter	Common Name	Scientific Name
1.	Humpback Whale	*Megaptera novaeangliae*
	Whale Barnacles	*Coronula diadema* *Coronula reginae* *Conchoderma quritum*
	Bottlenose Dolphin	*Tursiops truncatus*
	Killer Whale	*Orcinus orca*
4.	Krill—Antarctic	*Euphausia superba* *Thysanoessa macrura* *Thysanoessa vicina*
	Krill—Northern Pacific	*Euphausia pacifica* *Thysanoessa longipes* *Thysanoessa raschii*
	Herring	*Clupea harengus*
	American Sand Lance	*Ammodytes americanus*
	Capelin	*Mallotus villosus*
	Sperm Whale	*Physeter catodon*
	Blue Whale	*Balaenoptera musculus*
	Gray Whale	*Eschrichtius gibbosus*
	Fin Whale	*Balaenoptera physalus*
	Sei Whale	*Balaenoptera borealis*
	Minke Whale	*Balaenoptera acutorostrata*
	Right Whale	*Eubalaena glacialis*

 *Glossary*

baleen plates—a row of stiff material that hangs like teeth on a comb from each side of the upper jaw of a baleen whale

baleen whales—whales that have baleen plates and no teeth

barnacles—small crustaceans that attach themselves to surfaces such as whales or boats and form a hard shell

blowholes—a whale's nostrils; openings where a whale breathes in oxygen and breathes out carbon dioxide

blows—used here to mean a whale breathing out

blubber—a thick layer of fat beneath a whale's skin

brain flukes—deadly, wormlike parasites that may invade the brains of some kinds of whales

breach—a whale's leap out of the water

calf—used here to mean a baby whale

camouflage (KAM-uh-flahzh)—used here to describe a creature's attempt to disguise itself by looking like its surroundings

capillaries (KAP-uh-lehr-eez)—tiny blood vessels that connect arteries and veins

cow—used here to mean a female whale

crustaceans (kruhs-TAY-shuhns)—krill, lobsters, shrimps, crabs, and other mostly marine animals of a large class, Crustacea

cutting in—butchering a whale

diphtheria (dihp-THIR-ee-uh)—a severe disease caused by a certain bacteria and characterized in humans by weakness, fever, and the formation of a false membrane over the mucous membrane

dominance order—a series of relationships that determines the ranking of the members within a group of animals

echolocation—a method used by some kinds of whales to locate an underwater object by means of sound waves. The whale sends out sound waves that are reflected off the object and bounce back to the animal

endangered species (SPEE-sheez)—a species, or distinct kind of plant or animal, that is in danger of becoming extinct

escort—used here to mean an adult male humpback that accompanies a female humpback on the breeding grounds

extinction (ek-STINK-shun)—the death of all members of a species of an animal or plant anywhere on earth

feeding frenzy—nonstop eating

flukes—the flared end of a whale's tail

food chain—the flow of energy from producers to consumers in a community

habitat—the place where a plant or animal lives

krill—tiny shrimplike animals

magnetic field—an area affected by a magnetic force

mammals—warm-blooded animals with backbones and hair. The females bear live young and produce milk to feed them

migration—the seasonal movement of animals from one region or climate to another and back again for feeding or breeding

nutrients (NYU-tree-ents)—substances that promote the growth of living things.

parasites (PAHR-uh-sites)—harmful creatures that live in or on other creatures

photosynthesis (foh-tuh-SIHN-thuh-sihs)—the process by which green plants use carbon dioxide, water, and the energy from sunlight to make food

pod—used here to mean a group of three or more whales

prey—an animal that is caught and eaten by another animal

radio tag—a device that sends out radio signals. When attached to an animal, it is used to track the animal's movements

social sounds—used here to describe sudden, short bursts of sounds made by humpbacks, often followed by long silences. Social sounds are not repeated in long patterns

song—used here to describe the complex pattern of sounds created by humpback whales

species (SPEE-sheez)—distinct kinds of individual plants or animals that have common characteristics and share the same scientific name

streamlined—a shape that offers little resistance when moving through water

sound waves—a series of vibrations that travel through matter. When they reach an animal's ears, the vibrations can be heard as sounds

toothed whales—whales that have teeth

toxic chemicals—poisonous chemicals that in concentrated amounts can harm or kill animal and plant life

tryworks—a brick furnace used in removing oil from blubber

yearling—used here to mean a one-year-old whale

Selected Bibliography

Books for Younger Readers

Bunting, Eve. *The Sea World Book of Whales*. San Diego: Harcourt, Brace, Jovanovich, 1980.

Graham, Ada, and Graham, Frank. *Whale Watch: An Audubon Reader*. New York: Dell, 1983.

Shebar, Sharon Sigmond. *Whaling for Glory*. New York: Julian Messner, 1978.

Smyth, Karen C. *Crystal: The Story of a Real Baby Whale*. Camden, Maine: Down East Books, 1986.

Stein, R.C. *The Story of New England Whalers*. Chicago: Children's Press, 1982.

Books for Older Readers

Burton, Robert. *The Life and Death of Whales*. Second ed. New York: Universe Books, 1980.

Ellis, Richard. *The Book of Whales*. New York: Alfred A. Knopf, 1980.

Garrett, Howard, and Keays, Candice. *New England Whales*. Gloucester, Mass.: Cape Ann Publishing, 1985.

Leatherwood, Stephen, and Reeves, Randall R. *The Sierra Club Handbook of Whales and Dolphins*. San Francisco: Sierra Club Books, 1983.

Minasian, Stanley M., Balcomb, Kenneth C. III, and Foster, Larry. *The World's Whales: The Complete Illustrated Guide*. Washington, D.C.: Smithsonian Books, 1984.

Winn, Lois King, and Winn, Howard E. *Wings in the Sea: The Humpback Whale*. Hanover, NH: University Press of New England, 1985.

Articles

Baker, C. Scott, and Herman, Louis M. "Whales That Go to Extremes," *Natural History*, October, 1985, pp. 52-60.

Darling, Jim. "Source of the Humpback's Song: Giants Not Always Gentle." *Oceans*, March/April 1984, pp. 3-10.

Dolphin, William F. "Moods and Manners of Humpback Whales." *Animal Kingdom*, February/March 1985, pp. 40-45.

Evans, Michael. "Miracle Rescue." *Yankee*, November 1985, pp. 110-111, 200-203.

Gormley, Gerard. "Hungry Humpbacks Forever Blowing Bubbles." *Sea Frontiers*, September/October 1983, pp. 260-265.

Payne, Roger. "Humpbacks: Their Mysterious Songs." *National Geographic*, January 1979, pp. 18-24.

Nicklin, Flip, and Payne, Roger. "New Light on the Singing Whales." *National Geographic*, April 1982, pp. 463-477.

Steinhart, Peter. "In the Company of Giants." *National Wildlife*, April/May 1985, pp. 22-27.

Wehle, D.H.S., and Coleman, Felicia C. "Plastics at Sea." *Natural History*, February 1983, pp. 20-26.

"Whaling in America." *Cobblestone*, April 1984, entire issue.

Index

101, 114; "singing" of, 18-19, 21-23, 26, 28, 35

Humphrey: ancestors of, 111; birth of, 7-8; breeding grounds and, 34, 74, 83; feeding grounds and, 30, 34, 36, 62, 97; feeding season and, 35, 49-52; food for, 10, 62, 64, 66; migration of, 30-37, 74, 99; naming of, 85; relationship to mother of, 10-11, 15, 18, 20, 30-33, 35-37; rescue efforts for, 78-80, 85-89, 91-94; size of, 8, 35, 37, 80, 88; skin of, 9-10, 81-82, 92, 99; stranding of, 74-75, 79-80, 87-89, 91

hydrogenation, 111

International Whaling Commission, 113-114

kerosene, 107

killer whales, 16, 56, 66-68, 70

krill: definition of, 53; functions of, 56, 69-71; humpbacks and, 60, 62, 73; Humphrey and, 49, 52; salt content of, 54

Liberty Island Bridge, 80, 87, 89, 91

magnetic field, 38

Marine Mammal Protection Act, 83

minke whales, 57, 110

Nantucket, island of, 104-105

National Marine Fisheries Service, 74, 84, 89, 91

New Bedford, Massachusetts, 107

nutrients, 10, 17, 53

parasites, 81

photosynthesis, 53

pods, humpback: definition of, 16;

Humphrey and, 19, 51; number in, 27, 60, 62; size of, 30, 35; sounds of, 93

pollution, 54-56, 114

prey: humpbacks and, 58, 61, 70-71; number of, 37, 60, 69; trapping of, 53; types of, 35, 60

radio tag, 92

right whales, 57, 105, 107-109

Rio Vista Bridge, 79, 91

Sacramento River Delta, 75, 85, 91-92, 99-100

San Francisco Bay, 74-75, 81, 84, 94, 96

sei whales, 57, 110

Shag Slough, 80, 87

sharks, 16, 32

social sounds, 28, 61

sound waves, 38

species, 101

sperm whales, 56, 105, 107, 109-110

streamlining, 12

toothed whales, 56

toxic chemicals, 54-56

trying-out, 103

tryworks, 105

whales: hunting of, 104-105, 107-113; products from, 103, 107, 112-113; protection of, 101, 114; scarcity of, 105; types of, 56-57

whaling: Antarctic, 113; decline of, 107; methods of, 109; modern, 109; shore, 110-111; Yankee, 103-105, 107-108

yearlings, 16, 30, 35

 *About the Authors*

Carole Vogel and Kathryn Goldner have extensive experience as science editors, writers, and teachers and are the authors of two previous books for Dillon Press—*Why Mount St. Helens Blew Its Top* and *The Dangers of Strangers*. Teamed together since 1980, Goldner and Vogel have written hundreds of science activities and worksheets for a variety of elementary and secondary science textbook publishers. In addition, they have written numerous magazine and newspaper articles. They have also started their own educational consulting business. The dramatic story of a lost humpback whale and the efforts to save it prompted Goldner and Vogel to write *Humphrey the Wrong-way Whale*.

Kathryn A. Goldner lives in Wayland, Massachusetts, with her family. She attended the University of Wisconsin and graduated *magna cum laude* with a B.A. in biology from the University of Massachusetts.

Carole G. Vogel lives in nearby Lexington, Massachusetts, with her family. She graduated from Kenyon College with a B.A. in biology and received an M.A.T. in elementary education from the University of Pittsburgh.

052462

599.5   Goldner, Kathryn
GOL   Allen

         Humphrey the wrong
         way whale

    $11.95

	DATE		
	Dec.